D0409564

This
Dora the Explorer
Annual
belongs to
....
....

NICK JR.™

DORA the EXPLORER™

Annual 2008

Contents

EGMONT
We bring stories to life

First published in Great Britain 2007 by Egmont UK Limited, 239 Kensington High Street, London W8 6SA
Written and edited by Brenda Apsley Designed by Jeannette O'Toole

ISBN 978 1 4052 3175 6
3 5 7 9 10 8 6 4 2
Printed in Italy

I'm Dora, and this is my best friend, Boots. The world's a really fun place. Come and explore it with us!

Note to parents

Dora can help your child learn to speak Spanish. Boxes like the one below list English words, their Spanish equivalents, and a guide to pronunciation.

There is also a word list that begins on page 68.

Say it with Dora

hello hola say **OH-lah**

Hello, Dora!

Dora's seven, and she has lots of adventures. Clever Dora speaks English and Spanish. She'll help you learn, too!

Dora likes soccer. Her team is called Golden Explorers.

Do you like soccer?

Tick yes, *Si* ✔ or no, *no* ✗.

yes, *Si*  no, *no* 

Dora loves Osito, her teddy bear.

Do you have a teddy bear?

yes, *Si*  no, *no* 

Dora loves blueberries.

Do you like fruit?

yes, *Si*  no, *no*

Dora likes taking photos to put in her album.

Do you have a camera?

yes, *Si*  no, *no* 

Dora loves her pet puppy, Perrito.

Do you like animals?

yes, *Si*  no, *no*

Dora has lots of friends who help her.

Backpack goes everywhere with Dora. When Dora needs help, Backpack sings, "Anything that you might need, I've got inside for you." Sticky tape, umbrella, books: Backpack has them all!

Map lives in Backpack's side pocket. He peeks out when Dora says, "Map!" and tells her which way to go. He sings, "If there's a place you need to get, I can get you there I bet."

Dora's other special friend is - **YOU!** Will you help when she says, "I need your help!"? You will? Excellent! ¡Excelente! Write your name on the line.

....

Thank you, gracias.

Say it with Dora

yes	si	say **see**
no	no	say **noh**
excellent	excelente	say **ex-seh-LEN-tay**
thank you	gracias	say **GRAH-see-ahs**

Dora's friends

Boots the monkey is Dora's best friend. He's five, *cinco*, and loves making Dora giggle. He lives in a Treehouse, and is always on the go.

Boots likes:

- playing maracas
- bananas
- the colour red, *rojo*.

"I love my red boots!"

Isa the green iguana is six, *seis*. She lives in the Flowery Garden where she grows lots of flowers.

Isa likes:

- riding on her rocket ship
- playing the trombone
- Boots!

Tico the squirrel lives in a tree in the Nutty Forest. He's four, *cuatro*, and zooms around in his bicycle-plane and his little yellow car.

Tico likes:

- playing his harmonica
- nuts
- his stripey waistcoat

"¡Rápido, amigos!"

Say it with Dora

red	rojo	say **ROH-hoh**
four	cuatro	say **KWAH-troh**
five	cinco	say **SIN-koh**
six	seis	say **seys**

Benny the bull lives in a red barn with his grandma. He's six, *seis*, and he's big and strong.

Benny likes:

- his hot-air balloon
- playing his drum
- ice cream

"Oh, mannn!"

Swiper is a sneaky fox who lives on Blueberry Hill. He tries to swipe and hide the things Dora is looking for.

Swiper likes:

- riding his motor scooter
- dressing up in disguises
- flying around in his foxchopper

Dora's family

Dora lives with her family in a pretty yellow house, *Casa*.

My family name is Marquez.
What is your family name?

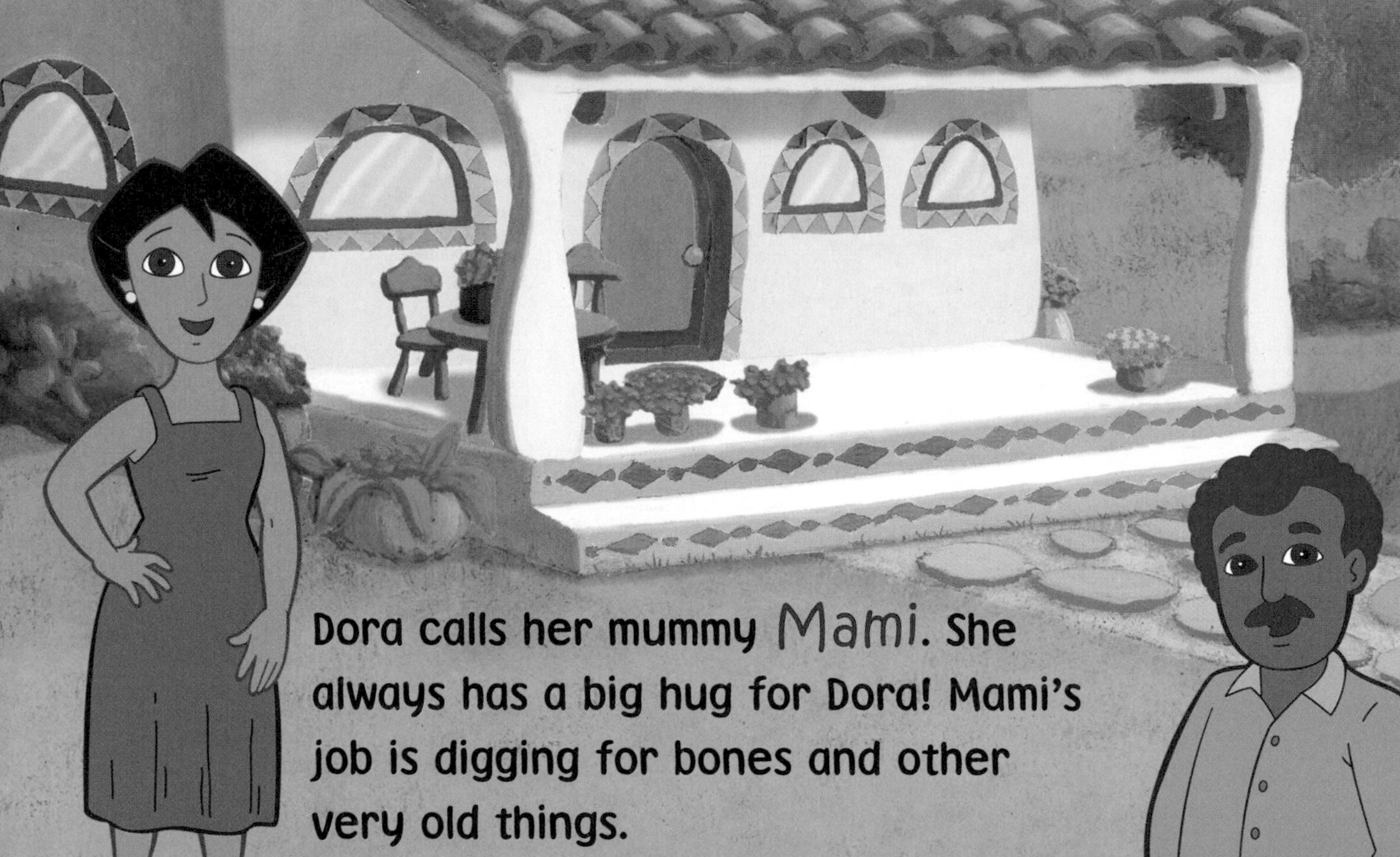

Dora calls her mummy *Mami*. She always has a big hug for Dora! Mami's job is digging for bones and other very old things.

Do you know what Mami's job is?
Clever you! Yes, she's an archaeologist!

Papi is Dora's daddy. He loves to cook, and he showed Dora how to make banana-chocolate-nut cake for Mami on Mother's Day.

Do you like making cakes?
Me too!

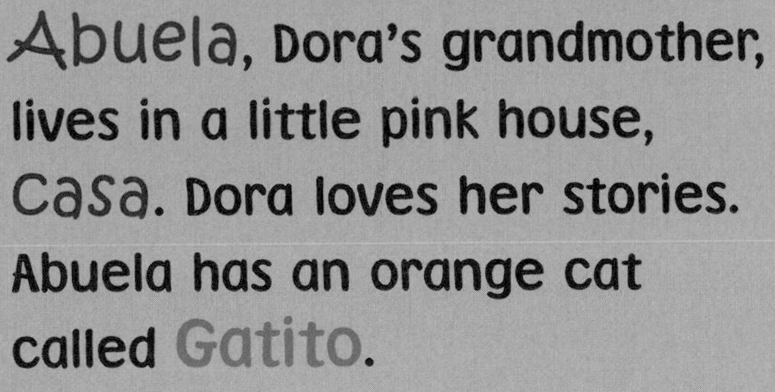

Abuela, Dora's grandmother, lives in a little pink house, Casa. Dora loves her stories. Abuela has an orange cat called Gatito.

What do you call your grandmother?

Dora's cousin, Diego, is eight. He lives in the Rain Forest and rescues animals that are in trouble.

Do you have cousins? How many?

Say it with Dora

house	Casa	say **KAH-sah**
Mummy	Mami	say **MAH-mee**
Daddy	Papi	say **PAH-pee**
grandma	Abuela	say **ah-BWEH-lah**

Baby Jaguar is one of Diego's animal friends.

All about Dora

Can you answer these questions about Dora and her friends? Look back to pages 8 to 13 to find the answers.

1 Dora's soccer team is Golden Boots.

True ✓  or false ✗  ?

2 Which of Dora's friends lives in the Flowery Garden?

3 What is Boots' favourite colour? Tick the answer.

red rojo  yellow amarillo  blue azul

4 This is Dora's cousin. What is his name?

5 Is Abuela's pet, Gatito, a dog or a cat?

6 Dora is five years old.

True ✔  or false ✗  ?

7 Which of Dora's friends has a hot-air balloon?

8 Who sings, "Anything that you might need, I've got inside for you"?

9 Who is this?

10 Who lives in Backpack's pocket?

ANSWERS: 1. false, her team is Golden Explorers; 2. Isa; 3. red, rojo; 4. Diego; 5. cat; 6. false, she is seven; 7. Benny; 8. Backpack; 9. Swiper; 10. Map.

Say it with Dora

red	rojo	say **ROH-hoh**
yellow	amarillo	say **a-ma-REE-yoh**
blue	azul	say **ah-SOOL**

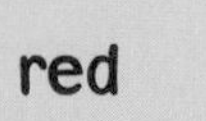

"Call me Mr Riddles!"

Hello! ¡Hola!
Do you like riddles? Boots does! He says, "Call me Mr Riddles!"
There's a contest at Tall Mountain to see who can solve the Silliest Riddle. But how will we get there?
Who do we ask for help when we don't know which way to go?

Map, that's right!
Map can tell us how to get to Tall Mountain.

I need your help.
Say, "Map" with me.

Map says first we go over the Troll Bridge, then through the Knock Knock Door, and that's how we get to Tall Mountain. Bridge, Door, Tall Mountain.

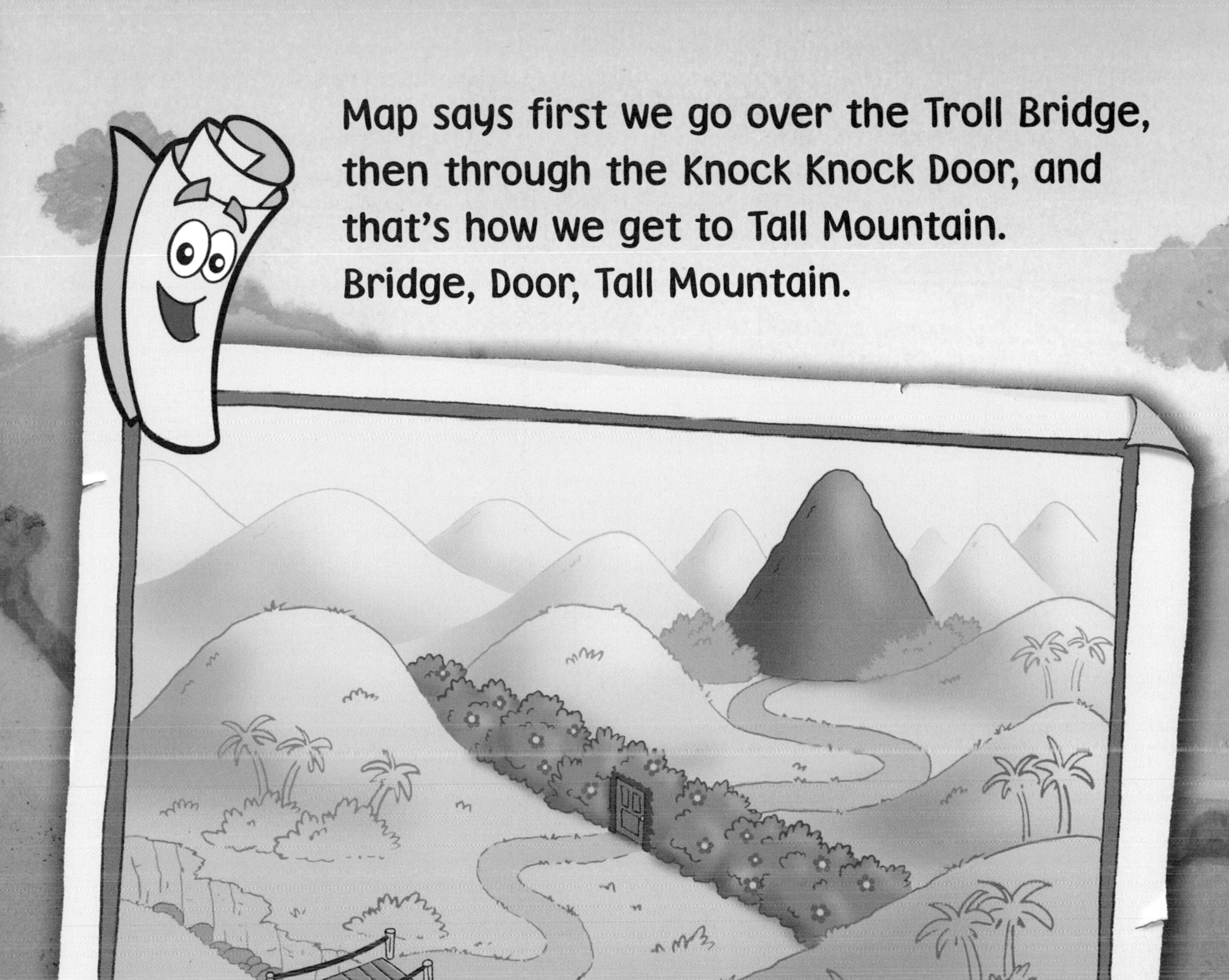

Say it with me. Bridge, Door, Tall Mountain.
Great! ¡Bueno!
Let's go! ¡Vámonos!

Say it with Dora

hello	hola	say **OH-lah**
great	bueno	say **BWEH-noh**
let's go	vámonos	say **VAH-moh-nohs**

Yes, we go over the Troll Bridge, then through the Knock Knock Door. Thanks for helping!

Look, do you see the Bridge? So do we! Let's go! ¡Vámonos!

Say it with Dora

let's go	vámonos	say **VAH-moh-nohs**
thanks	gracias	say **GRAH-see-ahs**

The Troll is grumpy. He says we have to solve this riddle to cross his bridge.
What has 8 legs and 2 tails?
Will you help us?
Thanks! ¡Gracias!

Let's stop and think. What has 8 legs and 2 tails?
Boots has 2 legs and 1 tail!

Here's Benny! He
has 4 legs and 1 tail.

Count with me. 1, 2, 3, 4, 5, 6 legs.

One, two, three, four, five, six.
Uno, dos, tres, cuatro, cinco, seis.

We need 2 more legs to make 8. Mine!
Let's count all our legs. 1, 2, 3, 4, 5, 6, 7, 8.

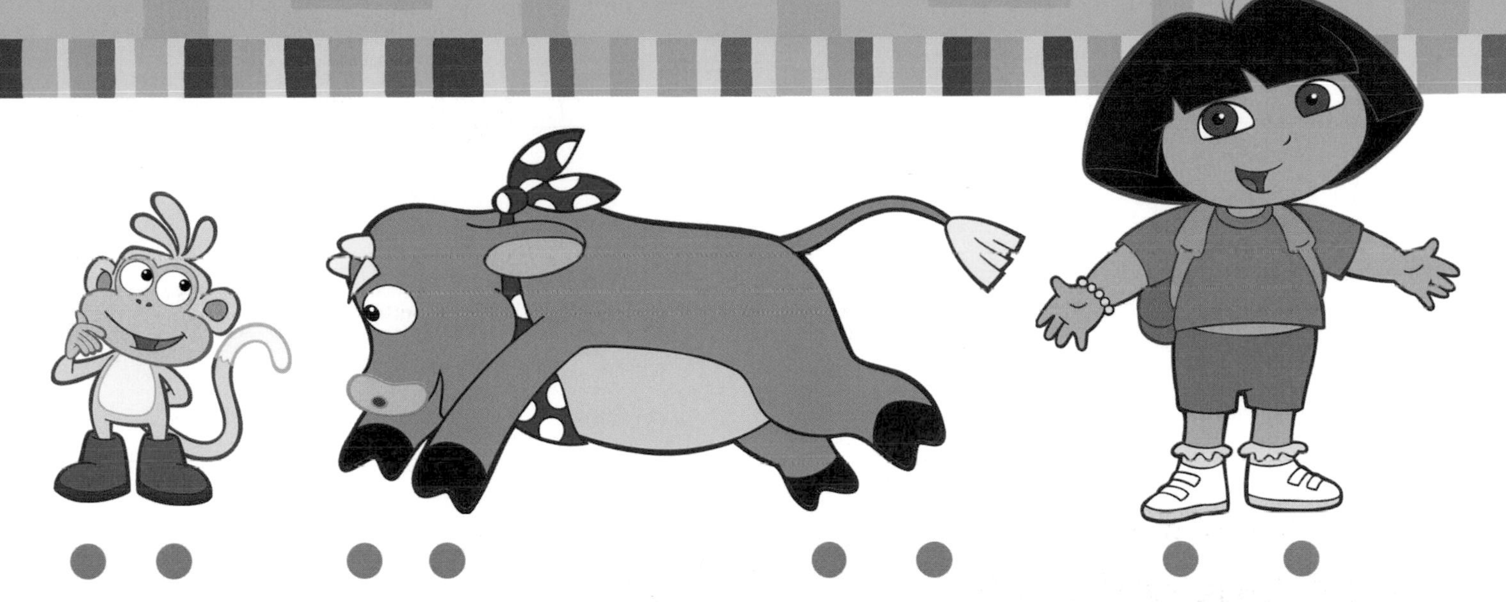

How many tails?

Yes, 2 tails.

8 legs and 2 tails. We solved the riddle! The Grumpy Old Troll says we can cross his bridge.
Thanks for helping!

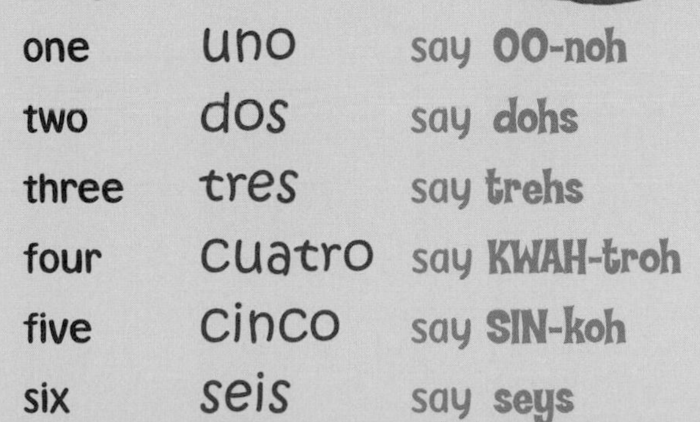

one	uno	say **OO-noh**
two	dos	say **dohs**
three	tres	say **trehs**
four	cuatro	say **KWAH-troh**
five	cinco	say **SIN-koh**
six	seis	say **seys**

Where do we go next? Do you remember?
Yes, Bridge, Door, Tall Mountain.
Right. Will you help us
find the door? Great!
¡Vámonos! Let's go!

Here's another riddle. Who is sneaky, and always trying to swipe our stuff?
Yes, Swiper the fox! If you see him, yell, "Swiper!"

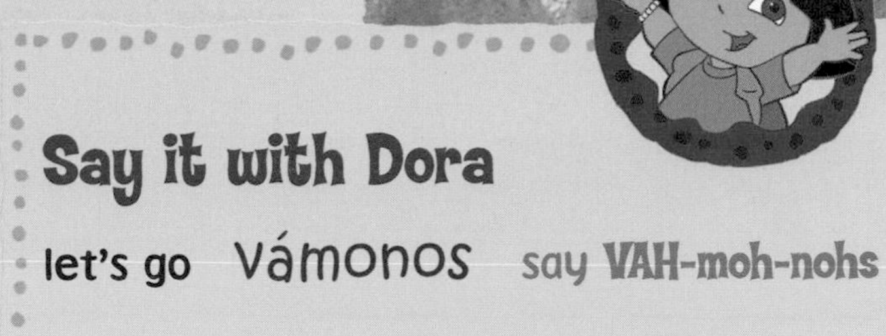

Say it with Dora

let's go Vámonos say VAH-moh-nohs

Help us stop Swiper taking our stuff.
Say, "Swiper, no swiping!" as loudly as you can!

Swiper, no swiping!
Swiper, no swiping!
Swiper, no swiping!

It worked! Thanks for helping us stop Swiper.

Here's the Knock Knock Door. The Knock Knock Door likes to tell silly jokes.
Will you help me knock on the Knock Knock Door? 1, 2, 3.

Now say, "Knock, knock!" with me.

When the door asks, "Who's there?", say, "Orange."

Then, when the door says, "Orange who?", say, "Orange you going to unlock the door and let us through?"

Yay! We couldn't have done it without you.

Where do we go next?
Bridge, Door, Tall Mountain. We went over the Bridge, through the Door, so next is Tall Mountain.

Do you see Tall Mountain?
Yes, there it is!
Let's go!

Here are some more silly jokes!

Knock, knock.
Who's there?
Noah.
Noah who?
Noah good joke?

Knock, knock.
Who's there?
Cock-a-doodle.
Cock-a-doodle who?
Who let that chicken in here?

Time for the Silliest Riddle. Who can jump higher than Tall Mountain?

Isa? No! Benny? No! Tico? No!

Let's stop and think.

Hey, mountains can't jump. But we can!

Let's all jump higher than Tall Mountain. You too!

Stand up, please. Now jump! Jump higher. Jump really high.

Hey, good jumping!

We can all jump higher than Tall Mountain because mountains can't jump!

We solved the Silliest Riddle! Well done, Mr Riddles. We did it! ¡Lo hicimos! Thanks for helping!

Dora's Happy Box

Dora has a Happy Box. It's where she keeps all the things she likes best!

Which of the things on this page are in the box on the next page?

Write a tick ✓ for yes, *si*. Write a cross ✗ for no, *no*.

Say it with Dora

yes	*si*	say see
no	*no*	say noh

ANSWERS: Numbers 1, 3, 5, 6, 7 and 10 are in the Happy Box.

Dora's photo album

Dora takes her camera, Cámara on all her trips. She takes lots of photos and puts them in her special album.

Dora took these photos of Benny. One of them is different. Can you find the odd one out?

Dora has lots of pictures of her best friend, Boots. Can you find 2 that are the same?

1

2

3

4

5

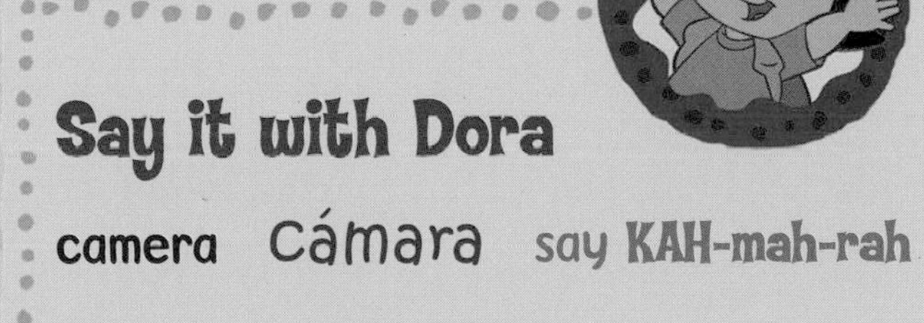

ANSWERS: Benny 2 is the odd one out.
Boots 2 and 5 are the same.

The Happy Old Troll

Hi! I have lots of things that make me happy.
Abuela made a blanket for me when I was a baby.
My bracelet was a birthday present from Mami and Papi.
What makes you happy? Can you see any things you like?

Say it with Dora

grandma	Abuela	say **ah-BWEH-lah**
Mummy	Mami	say **MAH-mee**
Daddy	Papi	say **PAH-pee**

My friend Boots makes me really happy.
Hey, where is he? Do you see Boots?
Yes, there he is, swinging on a vine!
That makes Boots happy.
We all have things that make us happy!

The Grumpy Old Troll is always grumpy.

Look at his grumpy face. Can you make a grumpy face?

Great face!

Let's find things that will make the Grumpy Old Troll happy.

Say the names with me, then we'll find them.

Flower and fireworks. Good! Where can we find them?

Who do we ask for help when we don't know which way to go?

That's right. Map! Say, "Map!"
Map says the things we need to find are in Play Park.
To get there we go over the Big Red Hill, then
across Fishy Lake.
Hill, Lake, Play Park.

Say it with me: Hill, Lake, Play Park.

I see a lot of hills. But which is the Big Red Hill?
Do you see it? That's right, there it is! Thanks for helping!
¡Gracias!

Let's climb up the
Big Red Hill.
Whoa! It's moving!

Say it with Dora

thanks gracias say **GRAH-see-ahs**

The Big Red Hill is really Big Red Chicken!
Say cluck, cluck, cluck, cluck! Cluck, cluck, cluck, cluck!
What's next? Hill, Lake, Play Park.
Yes, next we go to Fishy Lake.
Big Red Chicken will take us there!
Thanks! ¡Gracias!

Can you make animal noises? Say these with me!

cluck, cluck, cluck, cluck   baa, baa, baa, baa

woof, woof, woof, woof   moo, moo, moo, moo

Here's the Lake. Hello, Fish! ¡Hola!
Perhaps the fish will give us a ride
across the lake?
He said yes! Thank you! ¡Gracias!

Hill, Lake, Play Park. We went over the Big Red Hill
and across Fishy Lake.

So, next we're going to Play Park. It's up very high.
We need to find a way to get up there.
Our friend Benny has a hot-air balloon.
He says he can fly us up to Play Park.
That's great! Thanks, Benny!

Say it with Dora

hello	hola	say **OH-lah**
thanks	gracias	say **GRAH-see-ahs**

Hill, Lake, Play Park. We went over the Big Red Hill and across Fishy Lake. Now we're in Play Park.
Can you see the things that make the Grumpy Old Troll happy?
Point to the flower.
How pretty. Qué bonita.
Point to the fireworks. Wow!

We need to show the flower and the fireworks to the Grumpy Old Troll.

The Troll is going to be so happy! He'll do his Happy Dance!

The Troll is far away, so we need your help to call him.

Say, "Mr Troll!"

Louder. One more time. "Mr Troll!"

Say it with Dora

how pretty   qué bonita   say **kay bo-NEE-tah**

The Grumpy Old Troll is a Happy Old Troll now!
The flower and the fireworks made him happy!
He's so happy he's doing his Happy Dance.
Let's all dance with him!
Wiggle your arms - wiggle, wiggle, wiggle.
Now jump up and down - jump, jump, jump.
Hey, good dancing!

Say it with Dora

we did it	lo hicimos	say **loh ee-SEE-mohs**
thanks	gracias	say **GRAH-see-ahs**

We did it! ¡Lo hicimos!
We made the Troll happy.
We had a happy trip.
What was your favourite part?
I liked that too.
¡Gracias! Thanks for helping!

Spot the difference

These pictures of Dora and her friends look the same, but there are 5 things that are different in picture 2. Can you spot them all?

ANSWERS: 1. One of Dora's balloons is now pink;
2. Tico's tail is missing; 3. Swiper has gone;
4. A heart has appeared on Boots' balloon;
5. Benny has an extra scoop of ice cream.

Abuela's house

You can help read this story. Listen to the words and when you come to a picture, say the name.

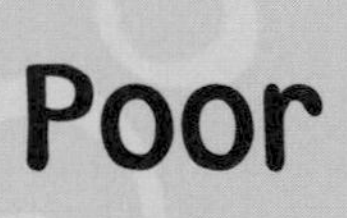 Poor  ! She's ill.  gives  and  a basket of treats to take to her.  tells  which way to go. “OK, Bridge, River,  's house,” says  . “Let's go!”

On the way,  and  hear a noise. Who is it? Oh, no! It's  the fox! ", no swiping!" say  and . It works! Naughty  runs away.  and  go over the Bumpy Bridge. Bump! Oh, no!  drops the basket!  gives  a fishing pole to get it. "Thanks, ," says .

"So next we need to find a way to cross Turtle River." The turtles make a path across the river for  and  to walk on. "Thanks, turtles!" says . "¡Gracias!"

"De nada," say the turtles.

"You're welcome, ."

"Where to next?" says .

"Bridge, River, 's house. We went over the Bridge, across Turtle River,

so next is ...  's house."

When  and  get there,

they see  at the front door.

 and  give her the treats.

"¡Gracias! Thank you!" says  .

She feels much better already!

Say it with Dora

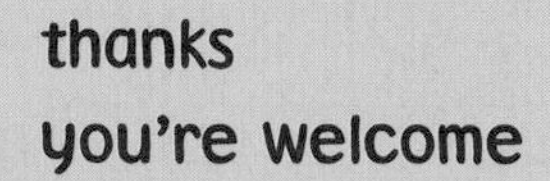

thanks	gracias	say **GRAH-see-ahs**
you're welcome	de nada	say **deh NAH-dah**

The Turtle River game

The turtles made a path so that Dora and Boots could cross Turtle River. Clever turtles!

Play this game with a friend. One of you is Dora and one of you is Boots. Who will get across the river first?

You need a dice and 2 counters (coins or buttons).

- Put your counters on **START**.
- Take turns to roll the dice. If you roll 2, move 2 turtles, and so on.
- If you land on a flower, have an extra turn.
- If you land on Swiper, go back to the start.

The winner is the first one to cross the river!

START
1
2
3
4
5
6
7
8
9
10
11
12
13
14
15
16
17
18
19
20
FINISH

Hide and seek

Hello! ¡Hola!
Here's Señor Tucán. He says that if we play hide and seek and find our friends, we can win the Big Trophy!
Will you play with us? Great! ¡Bueno!
Let's play!

Who is going be IT, and look for us? You?
Good, you can be IT! Thanks!
Count, so we have time to hide.
Put your hands over your eyes. Count with me.
1, 2, 3. One, two, three. Uno, dos, tres.
Now come and find us!

Say it with Dora
hello hola say OH-lah
great bueno say BWEH-noh
one uno say OO-noh
two dos say dohs
three tres say trehs

Where am I? Can you see me?
Yay, you found me hiding
behind the flowers!

What colour are the flowers I hid behind?
Tick ✔ the right flower.

Yes, they're pink, rosado. Good work!
Now let's find Boots! I'll help you look for him.

Where is Boots hiding?
Can you see him? You can?
Yes, the red fruit helped hide
his red boots. Red, rojo.
You're good at playing
hide and seek!

Say it with Dora

pink	rosado	say	**ro-SAH-doh**
red	rojo	say	**ROH-hoh**

Let's look for
our other friends.
Can you see Backpack
and Map?

Yeah, there they are! We found them!
You're really good at this game.

Which way should we go?
Who do we ask for help when
we don't know which way to go?

Map!
Say, "Map."

Map says that first we look in the Spooky Cave. Then we search the Squirrel Trees and then the Rain Forest. Cave, Trees, Rain Forest.

Are you ready to help find our friends? Come on!

First we must look in the Spooky Cave.
Can you see who's hiding there?

Yes, Benny is hiding there behind the rocks.
Who else is in the Spooky Cave?
It's a bear!
I think we woke him up. Let's get out of here!

We looked in the Spooky Cave,
so next is the Squirrel Trees.
Who's hiding here?
Yes, Isa and Tico!
One friend left to find!
Where is Señor Tucán?
Cave, Trees, Rain Forest.
Let's go to the Rain Forest!

The Rain Forest.
There it is! ¡Ahí está!
How will we get through
the big leaves?
Will you help us pull
the leaves apart?

Great! Put your hands out in front and pull to each side.
Pull and pull and pull and pull! Yay! Good pulling!

The tramcar will take us through the
trees, but first we need to climb up to it.
Tico will go first. Climb, Tico! Say, "sube."
Isa, Benny and Boots, you go now.
Say, "sube."
Now it's MY turn. Say, "sube."

We made it to the tramcar. Good climbing!
From the tramcar we can look for Señor Tucán!
You found him! Smart looking!

Say it with Dora

there it is	ahí está	say **ah-ee ESS-tah**
climb	sube	say **SOO-beh**

You found all our friends!
Can you point, and say their names?
Clever you! You won the Big Trophy!
We did it! ¡Lo hicimos!

We had fun playing hide and seek with you today.
What was your favourite part?
I liked that too.
Thanks for helping! ¡Gracias!

Say it with Dora

we did it	lo hicimos	say loh ee-SEE-mohs
thanks	gracias	say GRAH-see-ahs

"I see you!"

Boots is hiding from Dora! When she sees him, she calls, "I see you, Boots!"

Play with Dora. Which friends are hiding? When you see them, call, "I see you!" and say their names.

ANSWERS: Isa, Tico, Benny, the Grumpy Old Troll, Señor Tucán and Swiper are hiding.

Counting fun

Look at the butterfly, la mariposa.
He's bright blue, azul!

Will you count with me? Great!

1	2	3	4	5	6
one	two	three	four	five	six
uno	dos	tres	cuatro	cinco	seis

Can you help us count the butterflies?
How many green, verde?
How many purple, morado?

Oh, no, I hear Swiper! Can you help us find him?

Say it with Dora

butterfly	la mariposa	say **la mah-ree-POH-sah**
one	uno	say **OO-noh**
two	dos	say **dohs**
three	tres	say **trehs**
four	cuatro	say **KWAH-troh**
five	cinco	say **SIN-koh**
six	seis	say **seys**
green	verde	say **VEHR-day**
purple	morado	say **mor-AH-doh**
blue	azul	say **ah-SOOL**

ANSWER: There are 3 green butterflies and 5 purple butterflies.

Dora's word list

We've learned lots of new words! Say them with me.

English	Spanish	say
one	uno	OO-noh
two	dos	dohs
three	tres	trehs
four	cuatro	KWAH-troh
five	cinco	SIN-koh
six	seis	seys

I'm seven. How old are you?

Do you live in a house, casa?

English	Spanish	say
butterfly	mariposa	mah-ree-POH-sah
camera	cámara	KAH-mah-rah
house	casa	KAH-sah
toucan	tucán	too-KAHN

English	Spanish	say
Daddy	Papi	PAH-pee
Mister/Mr	Señor	say-NYOR
Mummy	Mami	MAH-mee
grandma	Abuela	ah-BWEH-lah

How many people are in your family?

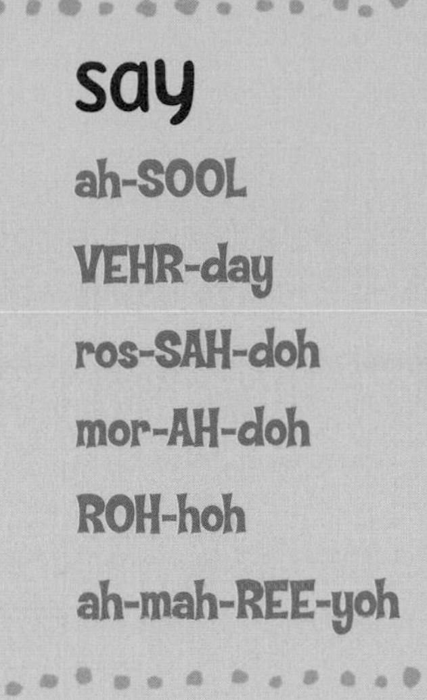

English	Spanish	say
blue	azul	ah-SOOL
green	verde	VEHR-day
pink	rosado	ros-SAH-doh
purple	morado	mor-AH-doh
red	rojo	ROH-hoh
yellow	amarillo	ah-mah-REE-yoh

I like pink, rosado. Which colour do you like best?

How many Spanish words do you know?

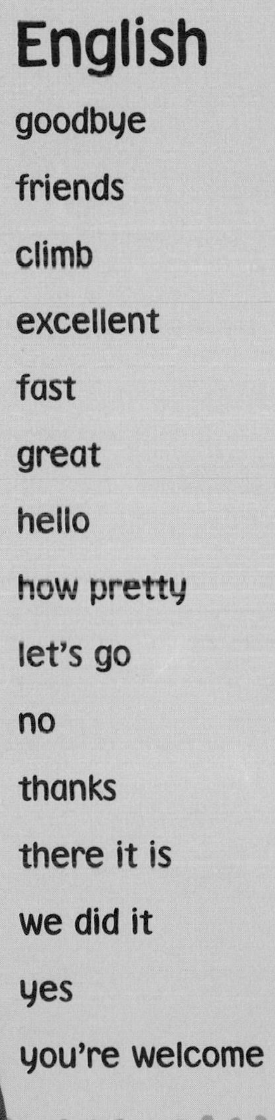

English	Spanish	say
goodbye	adiós	ah-dee-OHS
friends	amigos	ah-MEE-gohs
climb	sube	SOO-beh
excellent	excelente	ex-seh-LEN-tay
fast	rápido	RAH-pee-doh
great	bueno	BWEH-noh
hello	hola	OH-lah
how pretty	qué bonita	kay bo-NEE-tah
let's go	vámonos	VAH-moh-nohs
no	no	noh
thanks	gracias	GRAH-see-ahs
there it is	ahí está	ah-ee ESS-tah
we did it	lo hicimos	loh ee-SEE-mohs
yes	si	see
you're welcome	de nada	deh NAH-dah

Goodbye, friends! ¡Adiós, amigos! See you next year!